Ready Steady Read!

LEVEL 4

Dear Parents,

Congratulations! Your child has embarked on an exciting journey – they're learning to read! As a parent, you can be there to support and cheer them along as they take their first steps.

At school, children are taught how to decode words and arrange these building blocks of language into sentences and wonderful stories.

At home, parents play a vital part in reinforcing these new-found skills. You can help your child practise their reading by providing well-written, engaging stories, which you can enjoy together.

This series – **Ready, Steady, Read!** – offers exactly that, and more. These stories support inexperienced readers by:

- gradually introducing new vocabulary
- using repetition to consolidate learning
- gradually increasing sentence length and word count
- providing texts that boost a young reader's confidence.

As each book is completed, engaging activities encourage young readers to look back at the story, while a Picture Dictionary reinforces new vocabulary. Enjoyment is the key – and reading together can be great fun for both parent and child!

Prue Goodwin
Lecturer in

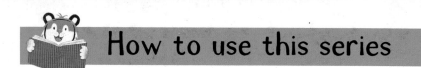

How to use this series

The **Ready, Steady, Read!** series has 4 levels.
The facing page shows what you can expect to find
in the books at each level.

As your child's confidence grows, they can progress
to books from the higher levels. These will keep them
engaged and encourage new reading skills.

The levels are only meant as guides; together, you and
your child can pick the book that will be just right.

Here are some handy tips for helping children who are
ready for reading!

Give them choice – Letting children pick a book
(from the level that's right for them) makes them
feel involved.

Talk about it – Discussing the story and the
pictures helps children engage with the book.

Read it again – Repetition of favourite stories
reinforces learning.

Cheer them on! – Praise and encouragement
builds a child's confidence and the belief in their
growing ability.

LEVEL 1 For first readers

* short, straightforward sentences
* basic, fun vocabulary
* simple, easy-to-follow stories of up to 100 words
* large print and easy-to-read design

LEVEL 2 For developing readers

* longer sentences
* simple vocabulary, introducing new words
* longer stories of up to 200 words
* bold design, to capture readers' interest

LEVEL 3 For more confident readers

* longer sentences with varied structure
* wider vocabulary
* high-interest stories of up to 300 words
* smaller print for experienced readers

LEVEL 4 For able readers

* longer sentences with complex structure
* rich, exciting vocabulary
* complex stories of up to 400 words
* emphasis on text more than illustrations

Once you have read the story, you will find some amazing activities at the back of the book! There are Excellent Exercises for you to complete, plus a super Picture Dictionary.

But first it is time for the story . . .

Ready?

Steady?

Let's read!

Nick Ward

The BIGGEST BADDEST WOLF

LITTLE TIGER PRESS
London

"I am the GREATEST!"
howled Harum Scarum.
"I am the biggest, baddest,
hairiest, scariest wolf
in the city!"

Harum Scarum looked at his
watch. "Time for some fun,"
he said. "But where's my teddy?"

Harum Scarum could not go anywhere
without his teddy.

"Ah! There you are!" he sighed.

First stop was the park.

"Run, little children, run, or I'll eat you up!"
he howled.

"Run, old people, run, or I'll eat you up!"
he howled.

"Eeek!" they screamed.

"Eeek!" they screamed.

Harum Scarum startled
a skateboarder . . .

petrified a builder . . .

and made a street juggler jump.
"This is fantastic fun," he cried.

But when he got home, he discovered that he'd lost his teddy!

"Oh no!" he said, frantically searching his room. But he couldn't find Teddy anywhere.

Harum Scarum crawled
sadly into bed.

The next morning Harum Scarum was
a nervous wreck.

"I must find my teddy," he wailed, and
hurried outside.

He looked high . . .

and low . . .

But Teddy was nowhere to be seen.

Finally he arrived at the bus stop.
"Excuse me, have you seen
a teddy?" he asked
the old people.

But they just tottered off shouting,
"Help! It's the biggest, baddest, hairiest,
scariest wolf in the city!"

Harum Scarum went to the park.

"Excuse me . . ." he began.

But the children rushed off shouting,

"Help! It's the biggest, baddest, hairiest,
scariest wolf in the city!"

Just then, Harum Scarum noticed a little boy, left playing on his own. And he was playing with . . . Harum Scarum's teddy!

"Please give him back," Harum Scarum whimpered. "I'm the biggest, baddest, hairiest, scariest wolf in the city."

"You don't look so scary to me," said the little boy.

"I'd do anything to get Teddy back," cried Harum Scarum.

"Do you promise to do what you're told from now on?" smiled the little boy.

"Of course," Harum Scarum said. So the boy gave Teddy back to Harum Scarum.

The next morning, Harum Scarum went
straight to the park.

"We're on the swings!" cried the
children. "Come and push us."

"Coming," smiled Harum Scarum.
He trotted up to the children . . .

"Run, little children, run,
or I'll eat you up!"

"Eeek!" the children screamed. "You promised to do what you were told!"

Harum Scarum chuckled. "You should NEVER trust the biggest, baddest, hairiest, scariest wolf in the city!"

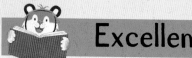

**Have you read the story? Well done!
Now it is time for more fun!**

Here are some questions about the story. Ask an adult to listen to your answers, and help if you get stuck.

Super Scary

Harum Scarum is the scariest wolf in the city but he can't go anywhere without his teddy! Do *you* have a special toy?

Amazing Imagination

Can you name some of the objects this picture? What kind of things do you have in *your* bathroom?

Messy Wolf

Now describe what Harum Scarum is doing in this picture.

Top Teddy

Can you remember if Harum Scarum finds his teddy?
Have *you* ever lost anything and then found it again?

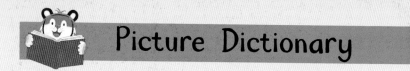

Picture Dictionary

Can you read all of these words from the story?

builder

city

please

run

scary

skateboarder

swings

teddy

tottered

wolf

Can you think of any other words that describe these pictures – for example, what colours can you see? Why not try to spell some of these words? Ask an adult to help!

Meggie Moon

Digger and Tiger spend all their time in the Yard. It's full of junk and it's their place. Then one day someone arrives, wanting to play . . .

Mouse, Mole and the Falling Star

Mouse and Mole are the best of friends. They share everything. But when a shooting star zips across the sky, they both want it for themselves. Could this be the end of a beautiful friendship?

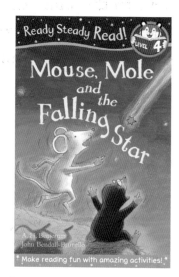

The Nutty Nut Chase

The animals are having a race! And the winner gets to eat a delicious, brown nut. But the race does not go as planned. And the nut seems to have a life of its own!

Robot Dog

Scrap the Robot Dog has a dent on his ear. So he is sent to the junkyard, with the other rejected toys. Will he ever find an owner?

For Bob and Sue — N W

LITTLE TIGER PRESS, 1 The Coda Centre, 189 Munster Road, London SW6 6AW
First published in Great Britain 2005
This edition published 2013
Text and Illustrations copyright © Nick Ward 2005, 2013
Printed in China
978-1-84895-678-0
LTP/1800/0603/0413
2 4 6 8 10 9 7 5 3 1

Books in the Series

LEVEL 1 – For first readers

Can't You Sleep, Dotty?

Fred

My Turn!

Rosie's Special Surprise

What Bear Likes Best!

LEVEL 2 – For developing readers

Hopping Mad!

Newton

Ouch!

Where There's a Bear, There's Trouble!

The Wish Cat

LEVEL 3 – For more confident readers

Lazy Ozzie

Little Mouse and the Big Red Apple

Nobody Laughs at a Lion!

Ridiculous!

Who's Been Eating My Porridge?

LEVEL 4 – For able readers

The Biggest Baddest Wolf

Meggie Moon

Mouse, Mole and the Falling Star

The Nutty Nut Chase

Robot Dog